A rose is red, the grass is green,
And in this book my name is seen.

____

Mother Goose Rhymes for All Times

Selected & Retold by
Corey Nash

Illustrated by
Leigh Grant

WARNER JUVENILE BOOKS
A Warner Communications Company
New York

For children of all ages
who believe in the magic
of Mother Goose.
C.N.

For Nicholas, Kyra,
Tony, and Claudia.
L.G.

Warner Juvenile Books Edition

Warner Books, Inc., 666 Fifth Avenue, New York, NY 10103
A Warner Communications Company

Printed in the United States of America
First Warner Juvenile Books Printing: September 1988
10 9 8 7 6 5 4 3 2 1

Library of Congress Cataloging-in-Publication Data

Nash, Corey.
Mother Goose rhymes for all times.

Summary: An illustrated collection of familiar Mother Goose rhymes.
1. Nursery rhymes. 2. Children's poetry.
[1. Nursery rhymes] I. Grant, Leigh, ill.
II. Mother Goose. III. Title.
PZ8.3.N29Mo 1988 398'.8 87-40699
ISBN 1-55782-055-4

Designer
Carlo De Lucia

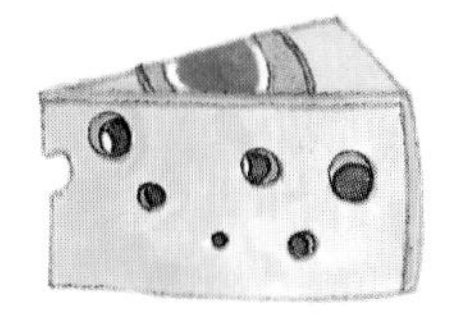

Contents

Hey diddle diddle,
The cat and the fiddle,
The cow jumped over the moon.
The little dog laughed
To see such sport,
And the dish ran away
with the spoon.

Hickery, dickery, dock,
The mouse ran up the clock.
The clock struck one,
The mouse ran down,
Hickery, dickery, dock.

What are little boys made of?
Snips and snails,
And puppy dogs' tails!
That's what little boys are
made of.

What are little girls made of?
Sugar and spice,
And everything nice!
That's what little girls are
made of.

Georgie Porgie, pudding and pie,
Kissed the girls and made them cry.
When the girls come out to play,
Georgie Porgie runs away!

Little Miss Muffet
Sat on a tuffet,
Eating her curds and whey.
Along came a spider,
And sat down beside her,
And frightened Miss Muffet away!

Pussy cat, pussy cat,
  where have you been?
I've been to London
  to visit the Queen.
Pussy cat, pussy cat,
  what did you there?
I frightened a little mouse
  under the chair.

I like little pussy, her coat is so warm,
And if I don't hurt her she'll do me no harm.
So I'll not pull her tail, nor drive her away,
But pussy and I very gently will play.

Jack, be nimble, Jack, be quick;
Jack, jump over the candlestick!

Wee Willie Winkie
runs through the town,
Upstairs and downstairs
in his nightgown.
Tapping at the window,
crying at the lock:
"Are the babes in their beds?
For it's now ten o'clock."

Pat-a-cake, pat-a-cake, Baker's man,
Bake a cake, as fast as you can.
Roll it and pat it and mark it with **T**,
And put it in the oven for baby and me.

Pease-porridge hot,
Pease-porridge cold,
Pease-porridge in the pot
Nine days old.
Some like it hot,
Some like it cold,
Some like it in the pot
Nine days old.
Spell me that in four letters.
I will: *T-H-A-T*.

Simple Simon met a pieman
Going to the fair.
Says Simple Simon to the pieman:
"Let me taste your ware."

Says the pieman to Simple Simon:
"Show me first your penny."
Says Simple Simon to the pieman:
"Indeed I have not any."

There was an old woman who lived in a shoe,
She had so many children she didn't know what to do.
She gave them some broth without any bread,
And then read them a story and tucked them in bed.

Sing a song of sixpence,
a pocketful of rye,
Four and twenty blackbirds
baked in a pie.
When the pie was opened
the birds began to sing,
And wasn't this a dainty dish
to set before the King?

The King was in the parlor
counting out his money,
The Queen was in the kitchen
eating bread and honey,
The maid was in the garden
hanging out the clothes,
When along came a blackbird
who nipped her on the nose.

Old Mother Goose, when
She wanted to wander,
Would ride through the air
On a very fine gander.

Three blind mice,
Three blind mice,
See how they run!
See how they run!
They all ran after the farmer's wife,
Who cut off their tails with a carving knife.
Did ever you see such a sight in your life
As three blind mice?

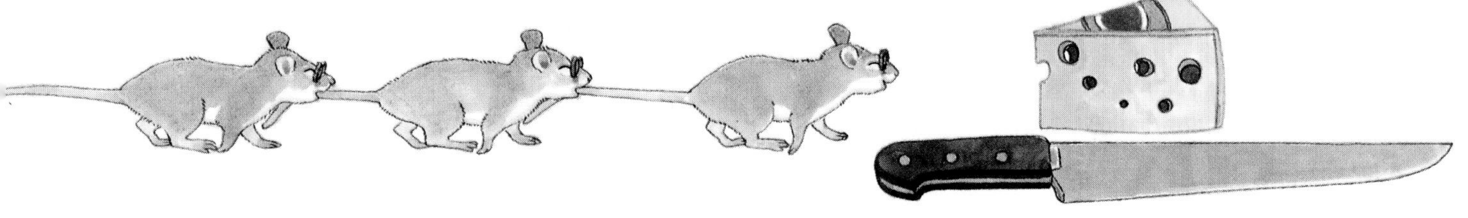

Little Bo-peep has lost her sheep,
And can't tell where to find them.
Leave them alone, and they'll come home,
Wagging their tails behind them.

Bah, bah, black sheep,
Have you any wool?
Yes, sir, yes, sir,
Three bags full.
One for my master,
One for my dame,
But none for the little boy
Who cries in the lane.

Mary had a little lamb,
Its fleece was white as snow.
And everywhere that Mary went
The lamb was sure to go.

It followed her to school one day,
Which was against the rule.
It made the children laugh and play,
To see a lamb at school.
And so the teacher turned it out,
But still it lingered near,
And waited patiently about
Till Mary did appear.

"Why does the lamb love Mary so?"
The eager children cried.
"Why, Mary loves the lamb, you know!"
The teacher then replied.

Jack and Jill went up the hill
To fetch a pail of water.
Jack fell down and hurt his crown,
And Jill came tumbling after.

Little Boy Blue,
come blow your horn,
The sheep's in the meadow,
the cow's in the corn.
Where is the little boy,
minding the sheep?
He's under the haystack,
fast asleep!

Will you wake him?
No, not I.
For if I do,
He's sure to cry.

Diddle, diddle, dumpling,
  my son John,
Went to bed with his trousers on.
One shoe off,
  and one shoe on,
Diddle, diddle, dumpling,
  my son John.

This little piggy went to market,
This little piggy stayed at home.
This little piggy had roast beef,
And this little piggy had none.
And this little piggy cried,
"Wee, wee, wee,"
All the way home.

To market, to market, to buy a fat pig,
Home again, home again, jiggety, jig.

Little Jack Horner
Sat in a corner
Eating his Christmas pie.
He stuck in his thumb,
And pulled out a plum,
And said, "What a good boy am I!"

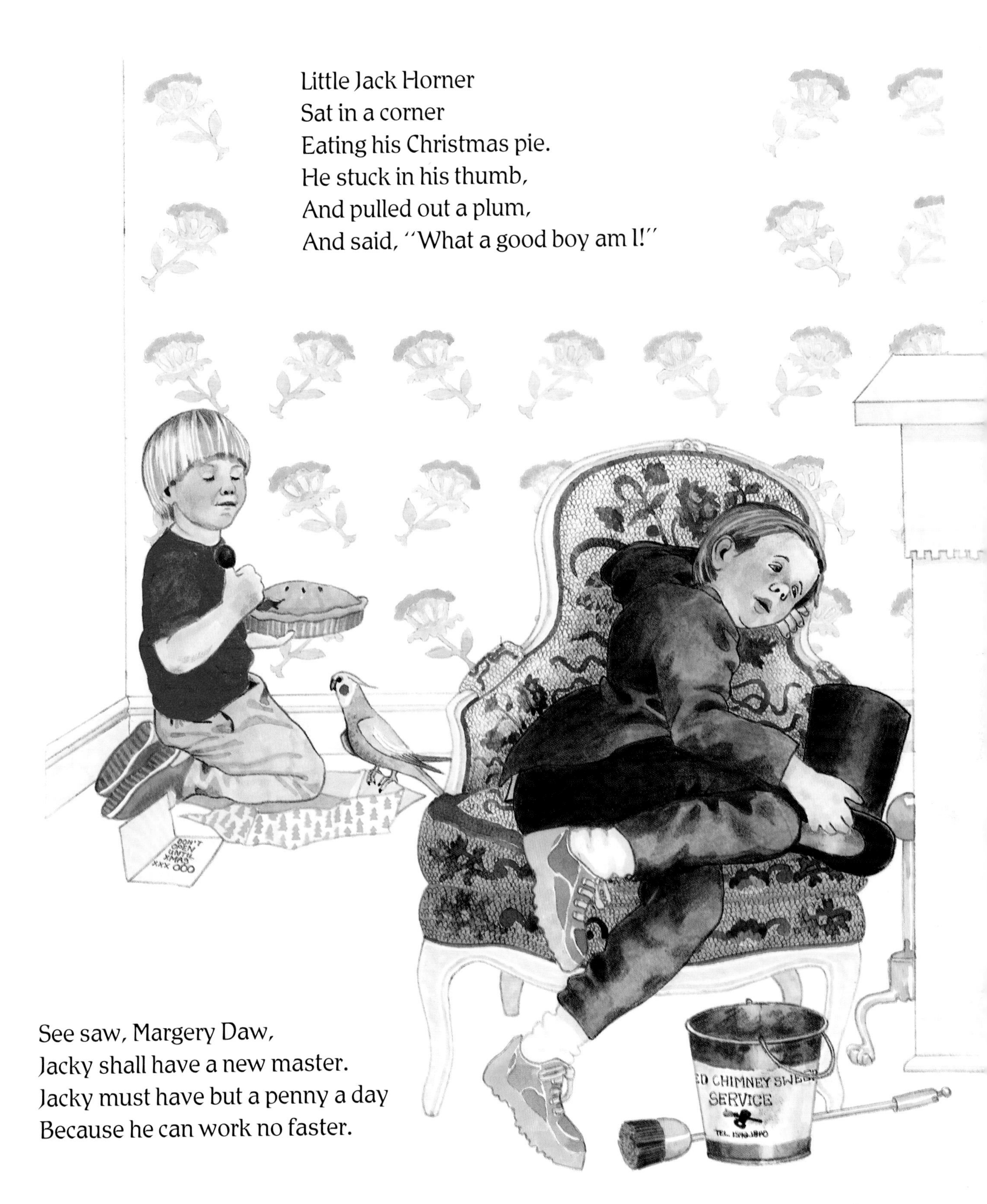

See saw, Margery Daw,
Jacky shall have a new master.
Jacky must have but a penny a day
Because he can work no faster.

Old woman, old woman,
  shall we go a-shearing?
Speak a little louder, sir,
  I am very thick of hearing.
Old woman, old woman,
  shall I kiss you dearly?
Thank you, kind sir,
  I hear you very clearly.

One misty, moisty morning,
When cloudy was the weather,
I chanced to meet an old man
  clothed all in leather.
He began to compliment,
  and I began to grin,
How do you do, how do you do?
And how do you do again?

Rock-a-bye, Baby, on the tree top,
When the wind blows the cradle will rock.
When the bough breaks the cradle will fall,
And down will come Baby, cradle and all.

Humpty Dumpty sat on a wall,
Humpty Dumpty had a great fall.
All the King's horses
and all the King's men
Couldn't put Humpty
together again.

Bye, Baby bunting,
Father's gone a-hunting,
Mother's gone a-milking,
Sister's gone a-silking,
And Brother's gone to buy a skin
To wrap the Baby bunting in.

Mary, Mary, quite contrary,
How does your garden grow?
With silver bells
  and cockleshells
And pretty maidens all in a row.

Old King Cole was a merry old soul,
And a merry old soul was he.
He called for his pipe,
And he called for his bowl,
And he called for his fiddlers three.

And every fiddler, he had a fine fiddle,
And a very fine fiddle had he.
The fiddlers sang,
"Tweedle dee, tweedle dee,
Oh, there's none so rare
as can compare
With King Cole and his
fiddlers three."

Old Mother Hubbard
Went to the cupboard
To get her poor dog a bone.
But when she got there
The cupboard was bare,
And so the poor dog had none.

As Tommy Snooks and Betsy Brooks
Were walking out one Sunday,
Says Tommy Snooks to Betsy Brooks,
"Tomorrow will be Monday!"

Rub-a-dub-dub,
Three men in a tub.
And who do you think they be?
The butcher, the baker,
The candlestick maker,
All jumped out of a fine potato!

Intery, mintery, cutery, corn,
Apple seed, and apple thorn,
Wine, brier, limber lock,
Three geese in a flock,
One flew east, one flew west,
And one flew over the goose's nest.

Yankee Doodle went to town
Riding on a pony.
He stuck a feather in his hat,
And called it Macaroni.

Cock-a-doodle doo,
The Princess lost her shoe!
Her Highness hopped,
The fiddler stopped,
Not knowing what to do.

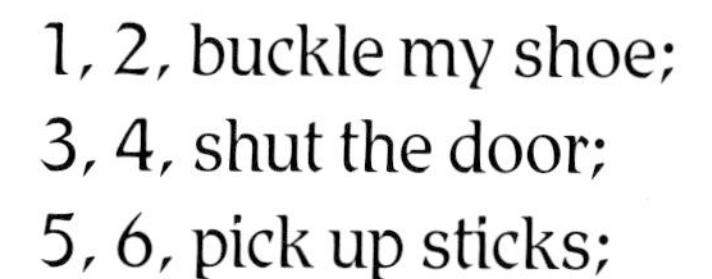

1, 2, buckle my shoe;
3, 4, shut the door;
5, 6, pick up sticks;
7, 8, lay them straight;
9, 10, a good fat hen;
11, 12, who will delve;
13, 14, maid's a-courting;
15, 16, maid's a-kissing;
17, 18, maid's a-waiting;
19, 20, my stomach's empty!

Higgeldy, piggeldy, my black hen,
She lays eggs for gentlemen.
Gentlemen come every day
To see what my black hen doth lay.

I bought a dozen new-laid eggs,
Of good old farmer Dickens.
I hobbled home upon two legs,
And found them full of chickens!

Handy Spandy, Jack-a-dandy,
Loves plum-cake and sugar candy.
He bought some at a grocer's shop,
And out he came, hop-hop-hop.

Little Tommy Tucker
Sings for his supper.
What shall he eat?
White bread and butter.
How will he cut it
Without a knife?
How will he marry
Without a wife?

The Queen of Hearts,
She made some tarts
All on a summer's day.
The Knave of Hearts,
He stole those tarts,
And took them clean away.

The King of Hearts
Called for the tarts,
And the King was mighty sore!
The Knave of Hearts
Brought back the tarts,
And vowed he'd steal no more.

A, B, C, tumble down D,
The cat's in the cupboard,
and can't see me!

A, B, C, D, E, F, G,
H, I, J, K, L, M, N, O, P,
Q, R, S, T, U, and V,
W, and X, Y Z.
Now I've said my A, B, Cs,
Tell me what you think of me.

Jack Sprat could eat no fat,
His wife could eat no lean.
So between them both
they cleared the cloth,
And licked the platter clean.

There was a crooked man,
And he walked a crooked mile.
He found a crooked sixpence
Against a crooked stile.
He bought a crooked cat
That caught a crooked mouse,
And they all lived together
In a crooked little house.

It's raining, it's pouring,
The old man is snoring.
Went to bed
Where he bumped his head,
And he didn't get up till the morning.

Rain, rain, go away,
Come again some other day,
Little Johnny wants to play.

Peter, Peter, pumpkin eater,
Had a wife and couldn't keep her.
He put her in a pumpkin shell,
And there he kept her very well.

Peter, Peter, pumpkin eater,
Had another, didn't love her.
Peter learned to read and spell,
And then he loved her very well.

Three wise men of Gotham
Went to sea in a bowl,
And if the bowl had been stronger,
This rhyme would be longer.

As I was going along, long, long,
Singing a comical song, song, song,
The lane that I took was so long, long, long,
And the song that I sung was so long, long, long,
And so I went singing along.